Goldilocks
and the Three Crocodiles

To Joni
From Zeyde Mick

For Sarah Massini
D. M.

First published in hardback in the United Kingdom by HarperCollins *Children's* Books in 2022

HarperCollins *Children's Books* is a division of HarperCollins*Publishers* Ltd
1 London Bridge Street, London SE1 9GF

www.harpercollins.co.uk

HarperCollins*Publishers*
1st Floor, Watermarque Building, Ringsend Road, Dublin 4, Ireland

1 3 5 7 9 10 8 6 4 2

Text copyright © Michael Rosen 2022
Illustrations copyright © David Melling 2022

ISBN: 978-0-00-850988-0

Printed in Italy

Goldilocks and the Three Crocodiles

MICHAEL ROSEN

Illustrated by DAVID MELLING

HarperCollins *Children's Books*

Did you know that Goldilocks had a dog?
Her dog loved talking.
Did you know that his name was Tiddles?
Tiddles loved walking.

Tiddles said to Goldilocks one bright morning:
"It's a nice summer's day.
We could see if we could find that house.
Do you know the way?"

"That house?" said Goldilocks. "What do you mean?"
"The house with the chairs.
There was porridge and beds. You went in. . .
there were THREE BEARS!"

So, Goldilocks and Tiddles
went walking through
a deep, dark wood.

Goldilocks chatted to Tiddles.

Tiddles chatted to Goldilocks.

Hmmm, thought Goldilocks,
where is that house?

The one with the chairs,

the porridge,

the beds

and the bears.

Where could it be?

Far off, Goldilocks and
Tiddles could hear something.
What was it?

It was the sound of the **sea,** coming in on the wind.

Tiddles could smell the sea.
"Hmmm," he said. "I love the smell of the sea."

"Do you hear that?" Goldilocks said.
"Yes," said Tiddles, "the sea is singing.
The sea is singing to US!
Come on! **Let's go!**"

At that, Tiddles set off, **running** and **jumping** . . .

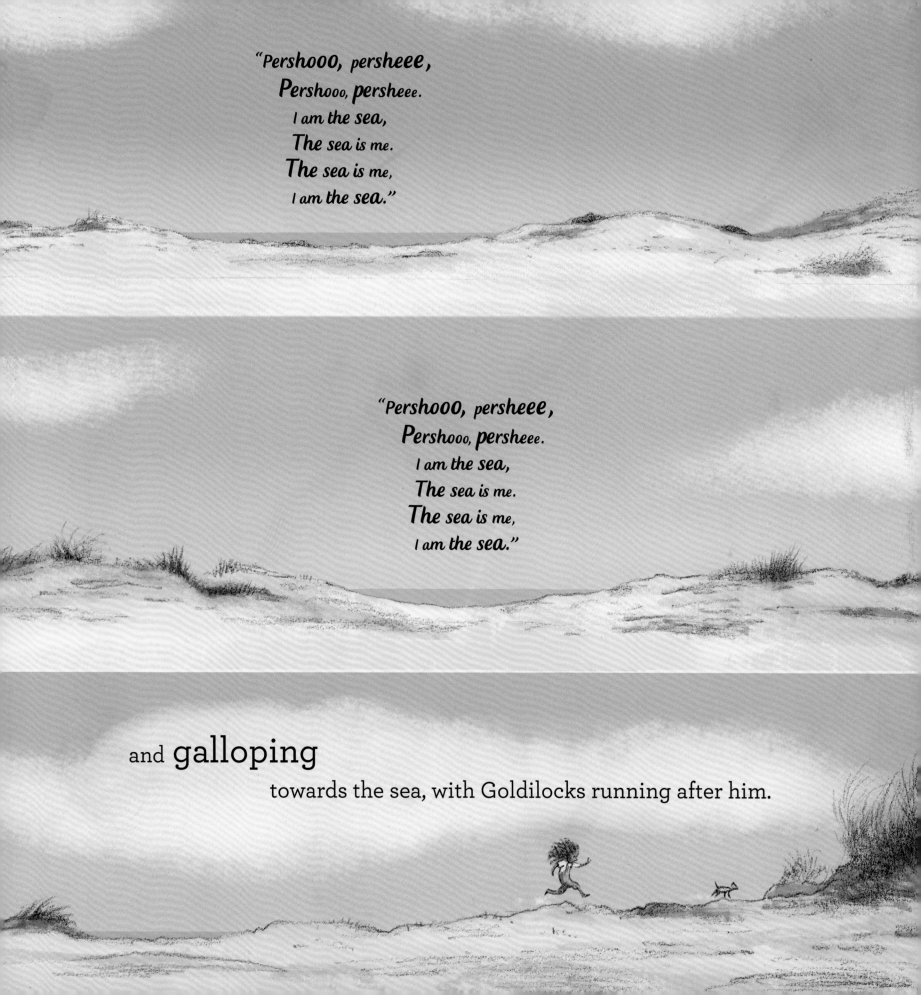

"Pershooo, persheee,
Pershooo, persheee.
I am the sea,
The sea is me.
The sea is me,
I am the sea."

"Pershooo, persheee,
Pershooo, persheee.
I am the sea,
The sea is me.
The sea is me,
I am the sea."

and galloping

towards the sea, with Goldilocks running after him.

Soon they got to a **beach.**
A long, long,
long, long,
long, long beach.
And now they could hear
the song even louder.

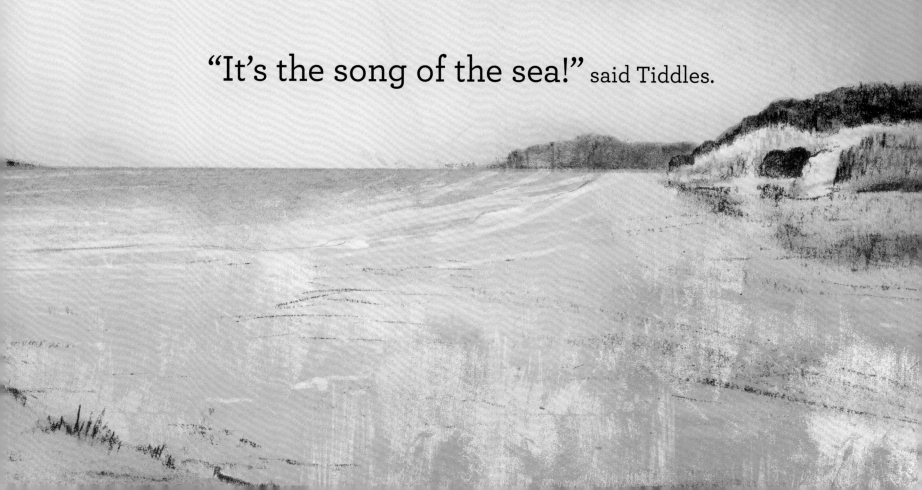

"Pershooo, persheee,
Pershooo, persheee.
I am the sea,
The sea is me.
The sea is me,
I am the sea."

"It's the song of the sea!" said Tiddles.

Up ahead was a **cave.**

A big, wide cave mouth ...

"Come on! Let's go in!" said Tiddles, and they ran towards the cave.

Slowly, slowly, slowly . . .

inside they crept.

Slowly, slowly, slowly . . .

and then they saw it . . .

. . . a table!

And next to the table there were **three chairs**.

Not ordinary chairs.

These chairs were **fish**.

Fish chairs!

Goldilocks hopped up and sat on one of them. Tiddles hopped up on to her lap. And it was –

yerchhhhhhhhh!

– much too slimy and slippery.

So Goldilocks sat on the next one. Tiddles hopped up and sat on her lap and –

yerchhh!

– it was *still* too slimy and slippery.

So Goldilocks sat on the next one. Tiddles hopped up and sat on her lap and –

ahh!

– it was just right.

On the table were **three bowls.**

And in the bowls there was **seaweed.**

Goldilocks tried the first one, and so did Tiddles, and it was –

phewwwwwwwwww!

– much too smelly!

Goldilocks tried the next one,

and so did Tiddles, and it was –

phewwww!

– still too smelly!

Goldilocks tried the next one,
and so did Tiddles, and –

ahh! – it was just right.

And they ate up all the
seaweed.

Crunch,

munch,

crunch,

munch.

Now Goldilocks was getting tired, so she looked round for somewhere to lie down and have a sleep.

There were **three huge** shells.
She got into one of them – *squeeze, squeeze, squeeze* – and all she could hear was the big, big, big, big, big sound of the sea.

*"Pershooo, persheee,
Pershooo, persheee."*

Too loud!

So she got out.

Then Goldilocks got into the **next** one, and she could still hear the sea but it was the not-quite-so-big sound of the sea.

> *"Pershooo, persheee,
> Pershooo, persheee."*

So then Goldilocks got into the **next** one . . .

and it was –

ahh! – just right.

> *"Pershooo, persheee,
> Pershooo, persheee.
> I am the sea,
> The sea is me.
> The sea is me,
> I am the sea."*

And it felt like she was going to sleep on the waves. And Tiddles felt like he was going to sleep too.

Lovely . . .

and off they went to **sleep.**

Then, all of a sudden, they heard a huge noise.

They heard someone say in a great big voice,

"Who's been sitting on my fish?"

They heard someone else say in a not-quite-so-big voice,

"Who's been sitting on MY fish?"

And then they heard a little tiny voice say,

"Who's been sitting on MY fish?

And it's all squashed!"

They heard someone
say in a great big voice,

"Who's been
eating my
seaweed?"

And then someone
else in a voice
that wasn't quite
so big,

"Who's been
eating MY
seaweed?"

And then they heard a
little tiny voice say,

"Who's
been
eating MY
seaweed?

And it's all gone!"

Then they heard someone say in a great big voice,

"Who's been sleeping in my shell?"

Then they heard someone say in a not-so-big voice,

"Who's been sleeping in MY shell?"

And then they heard
a little tiny voice say,

"Someone's been
sleeping in MY shell . . .
and they're still here!"

Goldilocks and Tiddles looked up . . .

. . . and they saw a . . .

…baby crocodile –

and behind the baby crocodile there was a

bigger
crocodile,

and behind that crocodile there was a

**huge,
enormous,
gigantic**
crocodile …

. . . and they were all going . . .

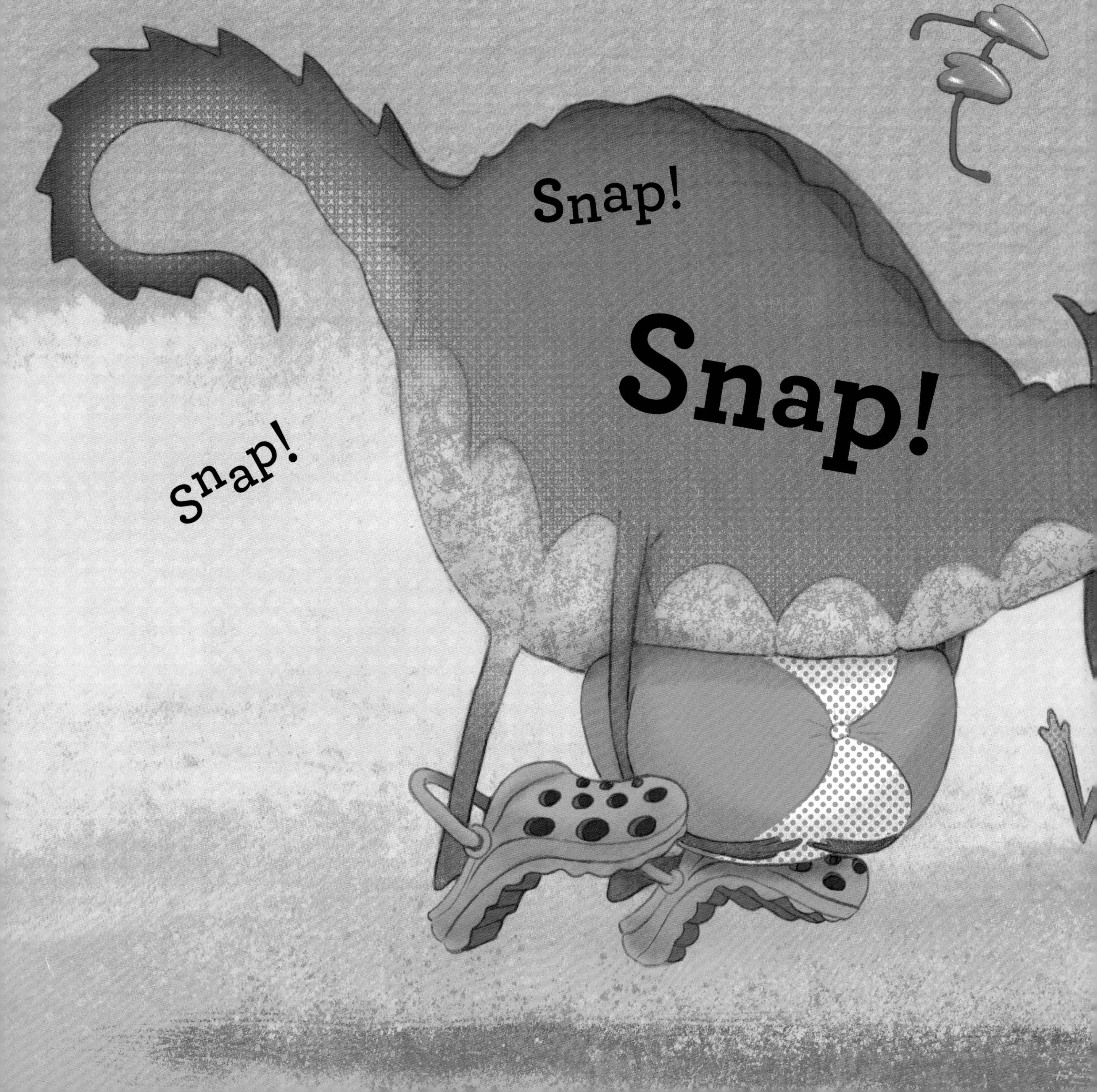

Goldilocks and Tiddles dashed out of
the cave as fast as they could . . .

along the long, long, long,
long, long beach . . .

through the
deep, dark woods . . .

and, and, and . . .

back home.

Later, when Goldilocks got into bed and Tiddles climbed up on to the bed too,
a **sound** came in through the window . . . that sounded like this:

"Pershooo, persheee,
Pershooo, persheee.
I am the sea,
The sea is me.
The sea is me,
I am the sea."